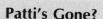
Patti's Gone?

"Lau-ren!" Stephanie said crossly, lurching to a halt.

"We have to talk," I said so seriously that Stephanie didn't make me explain myself, for once.

"Okay," she agreed. She turned to the tall seventh-grader she'd been dancing with. "Thanks for the dance, Andrew."

"Don't you think he's cute? *I* do!" she whispered to me as she followed me off the dance floor. "Did you have to cut in? I was having fun!"

"Sorry," I said, pushing her onto a folding chair and flopping down next to her. "But it's important. Have you seen Patti?"

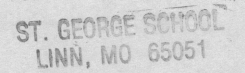

Look for these and other books
in the Sleepover Friends Series:

Where's Patti?

Susan Saunders

AN
APPLE
PAPERBACK

SCHOLASTIC INC.
New York Toronto London Auckland Sydney

ISBN 0-590-43190-0

Copyright © 1990 by Daniel Weiss Associates, Inc. All rights reserved. Published by Scholastic Inc. APPLE PAPERBACKS is a registered trademark of Scholastic Inc.

12 11 10 9 8 7 6 5 4 3 2 1   0 1 2 3 4 5/9

Printed in the U.S.A.   28

First Scholastic printing, August 1990

Where's Patti?

Chapter
1

"That must be it!" Stephanie Green exclaimed, peering through the window as the little plane went into a steep turn. "That must be Crab Island!"

"How do you know?" Kate Beekman leaned across Patti Jenkins' lap to stare out their window, too. "There are at least fifty islands out there!"

"Because it looks like a crab, of course," Stephanie said. "Can't you see it? Two claws sticking out of a round body? Also, there are all the sailboats clustered around it — the races must have already started. Wow! They're absolutely beautiful! All the different colors, speeding along making white stripes on the blue water. . . . You have to look, Lauren!"

"No way," I said firmly, still facing straight ahead. I'm Lauren Hunter, and being up in the air

1

with practically nothing under me makes me very nervous. If people were meant to fly, wouldn't they have wings? I swallowed hard as I felt the plane drop lower in the sky. "I'll . . . *ulp* . . . have a look when we're safely on the ground again."

"Water," Patti corrected me, since we were flying in a *sea*plane, about a thousand feet above the ocean off the Maine coast. Patti put down her book — her granddad had sent her a copy of *Birds of the Northeast* especially for the trip — and pressed her nose against the window she shared with Kate. "Hey, there's a lighthouse."

"And the village, and lots of dark gray cliffs," Kate added.

"And that has to be the Point, where we're staying!" Stephanie exclaimed. "See it, sticking out of the water? It looks like a crooked finger, or a crab's back leg! I can see three houses, too. I wonder which one is Nana's?"

Nana is Stephanie's grandmother, who used to be Mrs. Brinkman. Now she's Mrs. Kessler. She remarried not long ago. Stephanie, Kate, Patti, and I were visiting her and her new husband for the first time.

"And which house is the Tylers'?" Stephanie added curiously.

"It's not hard to guess what Stephanie has on her mind," Kate teased. She started humming that song of the Jangles that goes, "Boys, boys, boys! You can't live without them!"

"That's not *true*!" Stephanie sniffed. "Okay, so there just happen to be twin boys who are fifth-graders in the Tyler family, and Nana says they're cute. Big deal. In the third house on the Point there's a *girl,* and I'm just as excited about meeting her. I mean, I love Nana to pieces, but it'll be great having kids our own age to do things with. Don't you think?" Stephanie squinted out the window again. "The girl doesn't live on the island year-round, but her family comes out on the ferry practically every weekend."

"What if they don't like us?" Patti sounded a little anxious about meeting so many new people.

"Why wouldn't they?!" Stephanie asked, really surprised. She's not exactly shy in *any* situation.

"Sometimes kids don't like you just because you're new," Patti murmured.

Patti's had lots of experience being a new kid. She's had to change schools three times since kindergarten because her parents are always moving from one place to another to teach at different colleges. They're both history professors.

I can't imagine what that would be like, since

I've lived in the same place all my life. So has Kate. In fact, she and I are practically next-door neighbors on Pine Street, back in Riverhurst. There's only one house between us. So Kate and I started playing together when we were still in diapers. By kindergarten, we were best friends.

That's when the sleepovers began. On Friday nights, either Kate would sleep over at my house, or I would spend the night at hers. It got to be such a regular thing that Kate's dad nicknamed us the Sleepover Twins.

Not that there's anything very twin-like about Kate and me. We certainly don't look alike. She's small and blonde, and I'm tall with dark hair. And we don't act alike, either. Kate's very sensible, while I sometimes let my imagination run away with me. Kate's always early, I'm usually late. She's superneat, I'm on the messy side. I'm sort of a jock, while Kate would rather check out the action from the sidelines.

But in spite of all our differences — or maybe even *because* of them — we've never had a serious argument. At those early sleepovers, we'd dress up in our moms' clothes and play Grown-Ups, or School. Or else we'd make cherry Kool-Pops in the ice-cube trays, and melt s'mores all over the toaster oven, and call it "cooking."

As we got older, our sleepover menus definitely improved. Kate perfected her recipe for truly fabulous marshmallow super-fudge. And I invented my special onion-soup-olives-bacon-bits-and-sour-cream dip, which goes great with everything from Chee-tos to carrot sticks.

Kate's a real movie freak — she'd like to be a director some day — so as we got older we'd watch all the late movies on TV, or make up our own Mad Libs, or play Truth or Dare for Two. We'd spy on my older brother, Roger, and his friends, or think up ways to keep Kate's little sister, Melissa, from spying on *us*. And in all those thousands of hours we spent together we never had a fight . . . until Stephanie Green showed up at Riverhurst Elementary School last year. Stephanie's family had moved from the city into a house at the other end of Pine Street. I got to know her because we were both in Mr. Civello's fourth-grade class.

I thought Stephanie was great! She told terrific stories about the neat stuff she'd done back in the city. And she knew lots about fashion. She'd even already worked out her own style of dressing. Stephanie almost always wears red, black, and white, a combination that looks excellent with her black hair. Plus she was really funny. She had something to say about everything, and she made me laugh a lot with all her wild ideas.

I just *knew* Kate would like Stephanie as much as I did! So I decided to invite Stephanie to one of our sleepovers, so that she and Kate could get acquainted.

Major disaster! Kate said Stephanie was a complete airhead who could only talk about shopping and boys. And Stephanie told me Kate was a stuffy know-it-all. Neither of them wanted to see the other, ever again!

"The problem is obvious," my brother, Roger, said. "They're too much alike — both are bossy and *very* stubborn!" But I don't give up easily, either. Since the three of us live on Pine Street, I arranged it so that we all left for school on our bikes at more or less the same time in the morning. Once we'd survived that for a week or two, I managed to run into Stephanie, accidentally on purpose, at the mall a few Saturdays in a row while I was with Kate, natch. And when Stephanie invited me to a Friday sleepover at her house, I told her I'd absolutely have to bring

Kate with me, since we spent *every* Friday night together.

At the sleepover, Mrs. Green had made a platterful of yummy peanut-butter-chocolate-chip cookies, which are Kate's all-time favorites. Then we watched three movies in a row on Stephanie's private TV, which softened Kate up even more. The next time it was Kate's turn to have the sleepover, she agreed to ask Stephanie to come. And little by little, the Sleepover Twins became a threesome.

Not that Kate and Stephanie suddenly saw eye to eye, not by any stretch of even *my* imagination. Which is just one of the reasons I was glad when Patti showed up in Mrs. Mead's fifth grade this year, along with Stephanie, Kate, and me.

Patti's from the city, too. She and Stephanie were even in kindergarten and first grade together. But they couldn't be less alike. Patti's as quiet and shy as Stephanie is outgoing. She's also one of the smartest kids at school, and definitely one of the nicest.

Kate and I both really liked her right away. And when Stephanie asked if Patti could be part of our gang, we thought it was an outstanding idea. So school had barely started this fall, and *presto*! Now there were *four* Sleepover Friends!

The four of us do practically everything together. We know everything about each other, too, or *almost* everything. . . .

The seaplane gave a sudden lurch. "Yi-i-ipes!" I gripped both arms of my seat as tightly as I could and squeezed my eyes shut. "Couldn't we have taken the ferry, instead?!"

"How would we have gotten from the Portland Airport to the Crab Island Ferry?" Kate pointed out sensibly.

"Besides, Nana wanted to get us here as quickly as possible, so we'd have more time on the island. Four whole days and I don't want to waste a second!" Stephanie said. We had two extra days off from school plus the weekend because there was a big teachers' conference at Riverhurst Elementary.

My stomach suddenly took a nose dive. "Are we landing, or falling?" I wailed.

"We're *landing*, Lauren," Patti said soothingly. "We're skimming along close to the water. We're getting closer, closer . . . we're touching down!"

The pilot set us down on the water so smoothly that even *I* couldn't complain.

"Okay, it's safe to look now," Stephanie told me. "We're coasting toward the island . . . and there's Nana!"

I opened my eyes in time to see someone in a bright red coat — a liking for red must run in Stephanie's family — standing on a gray boulder and waving in our direction. Then the plane drifted to a stop beside a short pier, and the propellers slowly wound down.

The pilot climbed out of his cabin to open the outer door of the plane for us. "Thanks for flying Maritime Airways," he said as he helped us onto the pier. "Enjoy your stay on Crab Island."

Chapter
2

"Welcome to firm ground!" my stomach said. Waves lapped against the pier at my feet. The air smelled of salt, and seagulls were screaming overhead.

"I think that's a shearwater! Or a jaeger!" Patti said excitedly, whipping the bird book out of her jacket pocket again, and flipping through the pages.

"Patti, you have to promise you're not going to have your nose stuck in that book the whole time," Stephanie scolded. "We're here to have *fun*, not watch birds. . . ."

I took a deep breath of the clear, cool air and had a quick look around. Crab Island sloped up gently in front of us, ending in a hump crowned with tall pines. Little white wooden houses were scattered here and there among the trees.

Then Nana hurried from around a weather-beaten fishing shack and down the pier toward us. "Stephanie, dear!" she exclaimed, giving her grand-daughter a big hug and a kiss. She kissed Patti, Kate, and me, too. "You girls certainly are a sight for sore eyes. How was your trip?"

"Fine, except for Lauren's stomach," Kate said, poking me with her elbow.

"Piece of cake," Stephanie said. "After all, we had Dad with us from Riverhurst to Portland." Mr. Green is a lawyer, and he had had an early-morning meeting with a client in Portland. "He put us on the seaplane and forty-five minutes later, here we are! Brrr!" Stephanie shivered. "It's *cold*!"

"This is warm weather for Maine," her grand-mother said with a smile. "Come on! That's our car."

We grabbed our suitcases off the pier where the pilot was lining them up, and followed Nana to a shiny black Jeep station wagon that was waiting on the pebbled beach.

"Where's Dan?" Stephanie asked as we loaded into the car. Dan is Nana's husband, Mr. Kessler.

"He and Mr. Watson are racing the Watsons'

sloop," Nana said. "Mr. Watson's daughter is the girl I told you about, Stephanie."

Nana made sure we were all settled before she turned the car around and headed up a winding gravel road. "The girl's name is Mindy Sue, and she's —"

But Nana was interrupted by a major coughing fit from Patti, who was sitting in the second seat of the Jeep between Kate and me. Patti hacked and hacked — it sounded like she was choking to death! Kate and I pounded her on the back, while Nana stepped on the brakes and glanced worriedly over her shoulder. "I hope you're not coming down with something, Patti."

Patti shook her head. "J-Just a tickle in my throat," she mumbled, clearing it softly a couple of times. "Sorry."

"Are you sure, Patti?" Kate said. "That was some tickle."

Patti just shrugged.

"Are we going straight to the house?" Stephanie asked her grandmother when Nana had turned back to her driving.

"No, I thought first we'd stop by the village to see how Dan is doing. The whole island will be there, watching the races, so I can introduce you around."

"All ri-i-ight!" Stephanie said as Nana swung to the left at a fork in the road. The Jeep bumped from side to side over the narrow road.

"I'm sure you girls have noticed how rocky Crab Island is," Nana said.

She wasn't kidding about *rocky*! The island's practically all rocks, from enormous ones the size of our car, down to little stones no bigger than walnuts. Some of them were really pretty, but still . . .

"We do have one of the very few sandy beaches in Maine, though," Nana went on. "And that's where they'll hold the sand-castle contest on Sunday. They're having the kite-flying competition there, too, later this afternoon."

"That sounds like fun!" Kate said. The Beekmans have a collection of terrific kites that Kate's uncle sent them while he was traveling in Southeast Asia, so she's had lots of kite-flying experience.

"As a matter of fact, you're all entered in the competition," Nana said. "Dan ordered you a wonderful kite from a store in Boston."

"Excellent!" said Stephanie. "It'll be a great way to meet people."

"Like the Tylers, maybe?" I said with a giggle.

Stephanie made a face at me, but she couldn't resist asking Nana, "The Tylers *will* be there, won't they?"

"I expect so," Nana said. "The twins never miss out on anything. And they have an enormous silver kite. I've seen them flying it in front of their house."

We rolled over the hump in the center of the island, and down the far slope. In front of us, the village nestled next to the water between the two crab claws of rocky land. Its houses marched down the slope toward the harbor like stairsteps, and ended at a long, covered wharf.

Our gravel road ran right into the main street, which is one of the few paved streets on the island. It was decorated with lots of little colored flags, all flapping in the wind. A big banner stretched from the Crab Island General Store on one side of the pavement to the small post office on the other. TWELFTH ANNUAL SAIL-AWAY! BOAT RACES! CASTLES! KITES! DANCE! OLD-FASHIONED CLAMBAKE! it announced in large blue letters.

"A dance?" Stephanie said excitedly. Stephanie's a great dancer. "For kids, or for grown-ups?"

"We're all going," Nana assured her.

"And a clambake!" I said. I'm what you might call the serious eater of the group.

"That's right, on Sunday, after the judging of the sand castles," Nana replied.

"Do they serve anything besides clams?" Kate asked. "I'm allergic to shellfish."

"Roast chicken, hamburgers, hot dogs, baked potatoes, and more," said Nana. She pulled the Jeep into a parking space beside Jed's Garage and AutoParts. "Plus a wagonload of homemade pies, cakes, cookies — you name it."

"Sounds yummy!" I said, getting hungry just thinking about it. Kate and Stephanie call me the Bottomless Pit, but I tell them I just have a normal, healthy appetite.

"We'll walk down to the wharf," Nana said, opening her car door. "I've never seen the place so crowded!"

Crab Island's idea of crowded and Riverhurst's idea are two very different things. There *were* thirty or forty cars lining the street, but that's fewer than you'd see any day on East Main Street at home. The harbor was jammed with boats, though. There were small ones with rounded sides; boats with one mast — the mast is the pole that sails are attached to — and one sail; larger, one-masted-two-sail boats; ones with two masts and three sails; and even a three-masted schooner.

"It looks like the pirate ship in *The Jolly Roger*!" Kate said. *The Jolly Roger* is an old black-and-white adventure movie that Kate and I probably have seen at least fifteen times on "Film Classics" on Channel 6.

The wharf was plenty crowded, too. Nana introduced us to Miss Bessie, the postmistress. She said she never uses her last name, which seemed kind of strange to me. I mean, how do you think "Miss Lauren" sounds? We didn't meet any Tylers, but we did meet Jed McClintock, who owns the Garage and AutoParts, plus six or eight other islanders, while we squeezed through the mob to find some space next to the water.

As Nana explained to us, Mr. Kessler's race that morning was for sloops. They're the one-masted-two-sail ships with two crew members. For the race they had to sail out of the village harbor, between the two crab claws of land, then halfway around the island to the Point, where Nana's house is, and then turn around and sail back to the harbor again.

"Ship ahoy!" a skinny blond boy suddenly yelled. He had a great view because he'd managed to climb up to the roof of the wharf. In fact, he was hanging from the rafters by his knees!

"Look at that dope!" Kate said to the rest of us. "He's going to fall on his head if he isn't careful!"

"It's a yellow boat — the Keatons'!" the boy broadcast upside down.

There were cheers and clapping from the crowd.

Nana shook her head and sighed. "This is Dan's first race, and he was so hopeful about it," she said. "I hope he's not too disappointed."

"Another one's rounding the claws!" a second boy thundered from the rafters.

"If that guy falls, he'll . . . he'll bounce!" Stephanie giggled. He was redheaded, round-faced, and definitely plump, with big, orange freckles sprinkled across his nose.

"Way to go, Mr. Watson!" he hollered. Then he looked down and caught sight of us grinning up at him. And he made the most disgusting face I'd seen in a long time, pushing his nose up with one hand, and pulling his mouth down with the other.

"Ick!" Stephanie said.

"Very nice," said Kate wryly.

Patti nodded gravely, probably thinking that disgusting faces are often aimed at new kids.

"That's Dan's boat!" Nana was clapping her hands together. "Hurry! Hurry!"

The green boat *was* hurrying. The wind filled its sails and pushed it along until it seemed to be barely skimming the water.

"Let's go, Mr. Kessler!" Patti and I shouted at the top of our lungs as the little boat gained on the yellow sloop. "I'd love to learn to sail," I added in a lower voice. "It looks neat."

Kate was less enthusiastic. "Why are they leaning out over the edge of the boat like that?" she asked Nana doubtfully. The only parts of Mr. Kessler and his partner that seemed to be attached to the sloop were their feet. All the rest of them was hanging over one side! "Isn't it dangerous?" she added.

"Not really," Nana said. "They do that so the wind won't push the boat over. They're balancing the force of the wind in the sails with their own weight. Come on, Dan!"

"They're almost to the finish line!" someone announced from behind us. The finish line was a big red buoy bobbing up and down in the middle of the harbor.

"Yep. I think the Keatons are going to take it!" somebody else hollered.

Sure enough, the yellow boat slid past the red buoy only a half a length ahead of Mr. Kessler and Mr. Watson!

Now more sloops swept between the curved claws and into the harbor. But the four of us and Nana pushed back through the crowd and hurried to the dock to meet Dan and Mr. Watson.

Dan Kessler was already tying the green boat to a pier. He hugged each of us, and introduced us to Mr. Watson, who was busy coiling up ropes on the deck. He's a dark, stocky man with a bald head and a cheerful smile.

"You looked very impressive!" Nana said to both of them.

The two men grinned. "Thanks," Dan said. "Not bad for our first try, anyway."

"We'll win it next year," Mr. Watson said firmly. He jumped from the deck of the sloop to the pier.

Then a blond boy raced toward us, whooping and shouting. It was the same kid who'd been hanging from the rafters. "Good race!" he said, and leap-frogged onto one of the wooden piles.

And the redhead who'd made the face was right behind him! He gave the blond boy a shove, knocking him off his perch. Then the two of them started shadow-boxing around us!

"These guys are like out-of-control wind-up toys!" Kate murmured, and Patti backed up until she was safe behind Nana.

The redhead faked a karate kick at the blond boy. Then he said to Dan with a grin, "You and Mr. Watson weren't too bad."

"Not nearly as good as you two were," Dan said, separating them firmly. "Boys, this is my granddaughter, Stephanie Green. And these are her best friends, Lauren Hunter, Kate Beekman, and, over there, Patti Jenkins."

Patti waved awkwardly, still huddled behind Nana. She must be having a shyness attack, I thought to myself.

"Girls, these are our neighbors, the Tyler twins," Dan went on. Twins?! They looked about as much alike as Kate and me, although they did have a couple of things in common: their height — sho-ort — and their *attitude*!

"This is John," Dan said. John was the blond one — and he had freckles, too, only paler. "And this is Fred." That was the round-faced redhead.

"The *Tyler* twins?!" Stephanie murmured, wrinkling her nose. I had the feeling she'd been expecting something a little more glamorous than two short twerps with freckles and too much energy. . . .

I definitely agreed, and so did Kate, who whispered in my ear, "If Nana thinks *these* guys are cute, what must the other kids on the island be like?!"

I guess the twins weren't very impressed with us, either. They barely grunted a hello, and then they took up their boxing again.

But Dan went on admiringly, "John and Fred are terrific sailors. They won their race earlier today in an old, borrowed boat, with the wind against them!"

"Which gives us thirty points!" Fred said smugly over his shoulder.

"Points for what?" Kate asked.

John dropped his fists to answer. "The kid who gets the most points for the contests in this year's Sail-Away wins a brand new Sunfish!"

"What's a Sunfish?" Stephanie asked.

She got a horrified stare from both twins. "What's a Sunfish?!" Fred rolled his eyes, and pointed down the pier at a shiny little bright blue boat with a red stripe around the side. The boat had a single mast set right at the front. It was about twice as long as my bed at home, and twice as wide. And it looked like . . .

"It looks just like a toy boat I had when I was a baby!" Kate said, taking the words right out of my mouth.

"It's adorable!" said Stephanie.

"*Adorable?*" John groaned. "Give me a break!"

"For your information, landlubbers, that is not a toy!" Fred said sternly. "It takes an experienced crew of two to sail that Sunfish — and we're gonna be that crew. We'll never have to borrow a boat again!''

"That boat is ours!" John added, just in case we'd missed the point.

"Hold on. Do you mean they give points for the kite-flying contest, too?" Kate wanted to know.

"Yep," John replied. "We're entered in that, and in the sand-castle competition. We're gonna ace 'em all, take three firsts, and sail home in the neatest little boat on the island!"

"We're in those contests, too," I said. I meant it only in the friendliest way. I didn't care about winning a boat. Even if we knew how to sail, which we didn't, how would we ever get it back to River-hurst? Still, it was definitely the *wrong* thing to say.

"You know what I think? I think they shouldn't allow off-islanders to sign up for island contests!" Fred growled under his breath, just loud enough for Kate and me to hear. I was beginning to understand what Patti meant about being a new kid!

Kate looked like she was about to jump on Fred's case, but then Mr. Watson announced, "Here come Mona and Mindy Sue!"

A nice-looking, middle-aged lady in gray-striped slacks was walking quickly toward the green sloop. A brown-haired girl walked beside her. Mindy Sue is about my height. She's got long, straight hair parted in the middle, bangs, and you can tell she takes ballet because she has incredibly perfect posture. That day she had on a great-looking yellow wool cape with a hood, and bright green sweats. "Hi!" she said as soon as she was close enough. "You must be Stephanie and her friends! I've really been looking forward to meeting you!" Now, *that* was more like it!

"Hi!" Stephanie, Kate, and I sorted out which of us was who for Mindy Sue. Then we looked around for Patti.

"She was here a second ago," Stephanie said, puzzled. "Where'd she go?"

She wasn't behind Nana, or the wooden piling. She wasn't anywhere on the pier. Patti had disappeared!

Chapter
3

"Maybe Patti got cold," Kate said to Stephanie. "She might have gone somewhere to get out of the wind."

"Like back to the car," I suggested.

"Without saying anything to us?" Stephanie shook her head doubtfully. "That doesn't sound like Patti."

"Hey, Robert!" Mindy Sue suddenly called out. "That's Robert Tyler," she told us. "He's in high school."

"Wow!" Kate murmured.

"He's gorgeous!" I said under my breath.

"He looks just like Tommy Hepp!" Stephanie said. Tommy Hepp is our second-favorite TV star, after Kevin DeSpain. He's on *Roadies,* the new show about motorcycle cops, on Thursday nights.

I can't say that Robert Tyler really looked like Tommy Hepp, but he sure didn't look anything like his brothers! He was tall, with reddish-brown hair brushed to one side, big brown eyes, a golden-brown tan, and *no* freckles.

Robert waved a finger casually at Mindy Sue. "Hello, Mr. Watson, Mrs. Watson." He nodded at the Kesslers, too. But before anybody had a chance to introduce us, he said to his younger brothers, "Shake a leg, guys. Dad's waiting at the post office."

John and Fred groaned, but they didn't argue with him. Then Robert gave Stephanie, Kate, and me the briefest of smiles and hustled his brothers off the dock.

"Woooo!" Stephanie said to Mindy Sue. "Are you sure he belongs to the same family as those other two?"

"Maybe the twins will improve with age," Mindy Sue said hopefully. "Some people do."

"Six or seven years *is* a long time . . ." Kate said, which is how long it would take the twins to get to be Robert's age now.

"Ready for lunch?" Nana walked over to our group. Then she glanced around. "Where's Patti?"

"I think she must have gone back to the car,"

Stephanie told her grandmother.

"Oh," Nana said, looking a little surprised. She turned to Mindy Sue. "Would you like to come and have some of Dan's best beef-barley stew and homemade bread at our house?" she asked.

"I wish I could," Mindy Sue replied, "but Mom and I are taking Dad to lunch at the Home Port Restaurant, to celebrate his first race."

"See you later, then," Stephanie said.

"At the kite contest!" Mindy Sue smiled at all of us.

"I like her," Stephanie said as she, Kate, and I headed back to the Jeep. "She's really friendly, and she's a great dresser." Fashion sense is a big plus in Stephanie's book.

"Yeah, she's nice," Kate agreed. "It'll be fun to hang around with her. But what about those creeps, the Tyler twins?! I can't believe Fred practically *ordered* us to stay out of the contests!"

"You're kidding!" said Stephanie.

I tried to remember his exact words: " 'Off-islanders shouldn't be allowed to enter,' " I growled, imitating him.

"Well, in that case, we'll just have to *beat* them!" Stephanie said. "I don't care if they *are* our

26

neighbors! Hey, look, you guys. Patti *did* go back to the car."

Sure enough, Patti was sitting on the hood of the Jeep, her nose deep in her bird book.

"What happened to you?" Kate asked.

"Uh . . . I thought I spotted a fulmar, and I came back for my book to make sure," Patti said cautiously. A fulmar? But hadn't she stuffed the bird book back in her jacket pocket right after we landed on the island, when she'd looked up the shearwater, whatever *that* is?!

"More *birds*," Stephanie groaned. "Well, you missed meeting Robert Tyler. He's absolutely supremo! He looks *exactly* like Tommy Hepp. And Mindy Sue is terrific!"

"Oh. Really . . . " Patti mumbled.

Then Nana and Dan walked up to the Jeep, too.

"Patti, as soon as we get home, I'll lend you my binoculars," Dan said, catching sight of the bird book. He opened the car doors and exclaimed, "I'm starving! The sea air does it every time!" I knew what he meant. I felt like I could use a snack myself.

The four of us crammed into the second seat. Nana slid into the front seat next to Dan and he sped back up the gravel road and over the hump again.

He chose the fork we hadn't taken before, and in no time at all we were bumping out onto the Point.

"That's one good thing about the island being only six miles wide," Dan said with a grin. "You can get home for lunch in a hurry, no matter *where* you are!" Definitely my kind of place!

We rolled to a stop at the prettiest of the three houses on the Point — a wooden, two-story with silver-gray shingles. Then we piled out of the car and strolled up the flagstone path.

"All that carving is called 'gingerbread,' isn't it, Mr. Kessler?" Patti said.

"It certainly is," Dan replied. "This house was built in the last century, when people took the time to do all kinds of fancy handwork."

The gingerbread looked like white wooden lace, and it trimmed the edges of the roof, the windows, and even the door frame. Since the house sat at the tip of the Point, we could see the ocean in three directions from the wrap-around porch on the first floor.

Inside, it was cozy and warm. There was a big red enamel woodstove in the living room, and an *enormous* brick fireplace in the kitchen. The bedrooms on the second floor had white-washed walls and the floors were stenciled with flowers — roses, violets, and morning glories. Best of all, though, was the attic — the Kesslers had remodeled it just for us!

"Here's your room, girls," Nana said after we'd followed her up the two flights of stairs to the attic. "It'll give you some privacy, and we hope you'll treat it just like your rooms at home."

"Don't listen, Lauren!" Stephanie giggled, and covered my ears with her hands. I giggled, too. I can get pretty messy, and my room at home shows it.

But the attic room was too perfect to mess up — like the dream bedroom you always wish you had. It ran across the whole top of the house, with windows on four sides, and the sound of the waves everywhere. There was an antique brass double bed, a pull-out brown wicker couch, a handmade rag rug on the floor, and starched white lace curtains on all the windows.

Patti pushed the curtains back to stare out a window. "Which is Mindy Sue's house?" she asked Nana. That kind of startled me, since she hadn't even met Mindy Sue.

"The Watsons are farthest away from us, in that house with the tall fir trees around it," Nana replied.

"Oh," Patti said.

"And there are our next-door neighbors, the *Tylers*," Kate murmured, looking out another window.

"Where?!" Stephanie squeezed in next to her. "Oh, yuck. Those little jerks are *practicing*!"

Fred and John were in front of their house, flying a big delta-wing kite — the kind that is almost triangular. The Tylers' kite was silver, with a gold lightning bolt streaking across the middle of it. It was really up there, too, soaring almost as high as the highest gulls.

"Hmm," said Kate. "Looks like we've got *serious* competition."

The Tylers must have realized we were watching them, because all at once both of them turned toward us. Then they gazed up at the attic room, smirked triumphantly, and made a V for victory sign!

"Oh, yeah?!" said Stephanie. "I think they're a *touch* overconfident!"

"Yeah, we'll blow them out of the sky," Kate added grimly, "if it's the last thing we do!"

Chapter 4

We had a quick lunch. Dan's beef stew was great — I ate two bowls of it — and so was Nana's homemade Boston brown bread. Then Dan carried up our kite from the basement. It was a huge box kite, made of bright red Mylar — that shiny stuff that looks a lot like aluminum foil.

"All ri-i-ight!" Stephanie squealed. "It's fabulous, and my favorite color, too!"

"Very cool!" I said, and Patti added, "Like a modern sculpture!"

But Kate said, "I've never flown a box kite before," and she sounded a tiny bit worried.

"They're a little harder to get off the ground," Dan told us. "But once they're up in the air, you can't beat them!"

31

"Exactly what we wanted to hear!" Stephanie said. "Let's pack it into the Jeep and get going!"

The contest didn't officially start until two o'clock. But when we drove up to the edge of the sandy beach at about one forty-five, there were already twenty or so kites in the air. I spotted a few delta-wings like the Tyler twins'; and a few box kites like ours, only smaller. There were some of the regular diamond-shaped kind, with long tails, and even a swoopy Chinese dragon, made of twelve or so circles painted with scales, and hooked together with string. Lots of kids were dashing back and forth, gazing up at the sky or tugging on kite strings. But although I looked around, I couldn't find the Tylers or Mindy Sue.

"Should we try ours out?" Stephanie asked as we unloaded the box kite from the back of the Jeep.

Dan shook his head. "By the time you'd get it up in the air —"

"You'd have to bring it right down again," Nana finished for him.

So we took our time fastening the green kite string (which was rolled onto a big wooden spool with two handles that came all the way from India) to the kite in two places. We'd just finished when a tall, gray-haired man with a deep voice yelled for quiet.

"We'll be starting in five minutes!" he boomed through his cupped hands. "So get your kites back down on the beach, and get ready to go! There'll be prizes for the most unusual, largest, and smallest kites, of course. But *points* will only be awarded to the teams that get their kites up fastest and highest. Thirty points for first, twenty for second, and ten for third." He checked his watch. "Five more minutes!"

After that, there was a lot of scrambling around on the sandy beach as kids struggled to bring their kites back down without wrecking them or tangling them up. I spotted a few people we'd met at the pier, like Jed from the Garage in the village. He was with his two little girls and they were flying a tiny blue delta-wing with yellow stars all over it.

"You'd better get organized," Nana suggested, looking at her own watch. "There're only three minutes left!"

So Kate, our kite expert, took charge. "Lauren, I think you should carry the spool of string and do the running," she said in a no-nonsense voice, "since you're the fastest and strongest. There'll be a lot of pull on the string, because the kite is so large." I nodded, and picked up the spool.

"Patti, since you're the tallest, you'll hold the kite up in the air as high as you can while Lauren runs," Kate continued. "Stephanie will help you, and I'll trot alongside Lauren and give directions. Okay, everybody ready?"

"Only contestants on the beach! Only *contestants*!" the tall man hollered.

"Good luck!" Nana and Dan said.

"We'll keep our fingers crossed!" Nana added.

The four of us hurried away from the crowd of kids, and down the beach to stake our claim to some elbow room. But who should turn up right next to us? You've got it — the terrible Tyler twins!

"Is that the kite, or the box the kite came in?!" John hooted.

"You really think you're going to get that crate off the ground?" Fred added snootily.

"Just watch us!" Kate shot back, glaring at him.

Then the tall man shouted, "You'll have exactly fifteen minutes to compete! It doesn't matter whether or not your kite comes down during that time. If you can get it up again within the fifteen-minute period, do so! *Get ready . . .*"

Patti and Stephanie held our kite up over their heads, and Kate and I trotted away from them with the spool of string, until about twenty-five feet of beach separated us.

"Get set . . ."

The four of us nodded at each other, totally psyched to win.

"GO!"

I got a good grip on the spool of string with both hands, and started running. Kate jogged along beside me. "Faster, Lauren, faster, or we'll never get it to move! Hold the kite higher!" she yelled to the other half of our team, somewhere behind me.

"Hi! We're late!" Mindy Sue dashed past Kate and me with another girl. They were carrying a yellow diamond kite to a space farther down the beach.

Kate was quiet for a second, glancing over her shoulder. "I don't believe it!" she exclaimed at last. "Patti's disappeared again! Higher, Stephanie! It's coming, Lauren. Run faster!"

I ran. A big gust of wind blowing across the beach just then helped us out. Little by little, the box kite began to rise slowly into the sky!

At last I stopped running and turned to look at it. Huffing and puffing a little, I played out more string, a bit at a time, my eyes never leaving the kite.

But Kate was peering around at the competition.

"The Tylers' dumb delta-wing shot up like a rocket," she reported. "But don't worry. We're gaining on it. Mindy Sue's kite is pretty high, too."

"Where did Patti go?" Stephanie called as she ran down the beach to join us, her part of the job over.

I was too busy to think about anything but the kite. Box kites don't look like they're meant to fly when they're sitting on the ground. I mean, they look like skeletons of boxes! But once they're in the air, they really soar. And our kite was headed for the clouds. It looked beautiful — the red bands of Mylar gleaming in the sun like pieces of metal. I felt like cheering. We were going to win, I could feel it!

I could also feel the kite really tugging at the string. The wind was blowing harder now, great gusts shoving the kite first one way and then another. Not that the kite was about to get away from me — I had a good grip on that wooden spool! But there wasn't much I could do about controlling what was going on two hundred feet in the air!

"We're getting kind of close to the Tylers, aren't we?" Stephanie said all of a sudden.

I'd been too focused on our kite to look out for theirs. Anyway, I figured they were far enough down the beach that we wouldn't crowd each other. But now I spotted the Tylers' kite out of the corner of my eye, a silver triangle swaying dangerously back and forth in the wind just like ours was.

"Lauren, move away from them," Kate ordered. "Walk backwards with the spool!"

"I'm trying," I wailed, pulling on the spool as hard as I could. But it was no use. The kite was pulling even harder! In fact, it was actually dragging me a few steps *closer* to the Tylers!

"Get out of here!" John yelled, making shooing motions at me with his hands. Fred could only scowl, since he was the one actually flying the delta-wing.

"Lauren, I'll take over!" Kate said, reaching for the spool. That was a mistake. Kate's not nearly as strong as I am. The spool twisted in her hands as soon as she grabbed it, and what looked like miles of string played out before I could take it back!

"Oh, no!" Stephanie groaned, covering her eyes. "I think we're going to crash right into them!"

"AAARRGH!" There was a cry of total outrage from Fred. The wind had sent our kite straight into the Tylers' kite string! Fred started to run backwards, hoping to pull away from us before he got caught. But another gust of wind spun our kites around and tangled up our kite strings like wet spaghetti!

"SEE WHAT YOU'VE DONE!" John hollered, his face turning a deep, dark red.

"You've ruined everything!" Fred screeched.

Stephanie, Kate, and I stared helplessly as our box kite began to drag their delta-wing further and further down.

"When I said we'd blow them out of the sky, I sure didn't mean this way!" Kate mumbled.

"There's still some time left," Stephanie said, looking at her watch. "It's not the end of the world, guys. We'll just untangle the kites and send them up again, right?"

"Not unless you have scuba gear, you won't, " Kate replied glumly.

Because the falling kites missed the beach altogether. They dropped down on the water, floating for a moment on the crest of a wave. Then they slowly sank into the dark blue Atlantic.

I was about to say we were sorry when Fred slammed his spool down on the sand and glowered at us.

"Wow, Fred looks like Melissa, just before she has a temper tantrum!" said Kate under her breath. Melissa, Kate's little sister, is famous for her temper.

"Yeah," Stephanie murmured, "if looks could kill . . ."

Fred's face was even redder than John's, about the color of our poor ex-kite. He looked ready to explode! I was starting to think I might have to try out one of the fancy wrestling moves my brother, Roger, taught me, like the full body slam or the half nelson.

Then, luckily, the tall, gray-haired man in charge of the contest stepped between us and the Tylers. "Sorry you had such bad luck, Fred, John," he said heartily. "That wind is pretty tricky today. But I know you'll try again next year."

"Yes, Mr. Fenton," they mumbled.

"You, too, girls," Mr. Fenton said to Stephanie, Kate, and me. "Too bad about your kite going down. You were doing so well with it." Then he introduced himself. "I'm Howard Fenton, superintendent of the Crab Island schools. I'm an old friend of Dan Kessler's."

"Nice to meet you." The three of us shook hands with Mr. Fenton. I quickly looked around for Patti, but I didn't see her *anywhere*. Why had she just gone off like that?

"And I have some good news for you," Mr. Fenton went on. "Your first contest on Crab Island isn't going to be a total loss, after all. You girls will take home the trophy for the largest kite!"

I heard an outraged squawk from Fred and John. And as they stalked past us toward the parked cars at the edge of the beach, John hissed, "You'd better stay out of our way!"

"From now on!" Fred added.

I don't know about Kate and Stephanie, but I didn't like the sound of that. The Tyler twins versus the Sleepover Friends was one contest I *wasn't* having fun with at all!

Chapter
5

At least the trophy we won was nice. It was a brass statue of a kid flying a diamond-shaped kite with a long tail streaming down. TWELFTH ANNUAL SAIL-AWAY, the plaque on the bottom read. LARGEST KITE.

The little McClintock girls won the trophy for "Smallest Kite," for their tiny blue star-sprinkled delta-wing. "Most Unusual" went to the Chinese dragon kite, flown by two boys and a girl named Washburn.

A brother and sister, Josh and Becky Levy, won thirty points for having the fastest and highest kite, with a sleek orange delta-wing. Two brothers named Sam and Bob Baxter came in second. And Mindy Sue and her partner, Jane Pinter, placed third, which gave them ten points toward the Sunfish.

"Not that we have a prayer of winning anything else," Mindy Sue said, once the winners had been announced and the prizes handed out. "But third place is better than nothing, I guess."

"I love your trophy," Jane Pinter told us.

"It *is* nice," Kate agreed sadly, "but I really think we could have beaten the Tylers!"

"And now they're ready to throttle us!" I added, only half joking. I remembered all too clearly the look on Fred's face after the kites had disappeared into the ocean.

"Don't feel bad. The Tyler twins aren't exactly the world's greatest losers," Jane Pinter said. "There are so few kids on the island full-time that they're used to winning games almost all the time and when they don't . . . Remember last summer, when Harold Michaelson beat Fred in the swimming race around the Point, Mindy Sue?"

"Harold's from Portland, and John kept yelling that an off-islander shouldn't be allowed to compete," Mindy Sue said.

"That's what they told us!" I said.

"And Fred pouted for three whole weeks," Mindy Sue finished. "It was incredible."

Then she added, "I'm sleeping over at Jane's

tonight. But I guess we'll see you guys back here tomorrow morning, right?"

"Tomorrow morning?" asked Kate. "What's tomorrow morning?"

"Everybody starts their sand castles a day ahead of time," Jane explained. "You can't get much done if you leave it all until the last minute on Sunday morning."

"Then we'll see you tomorrow morning," Stephanie said.

We waved good-bye and started picking our way around the rocks and boulders that poked out of the beach between us and Dan's Jeep. I was starting to really wonder where Patti had gone, and *why*. And that's when we spotted her. She was sitting on the ground with her back against a wedge-shaped rock.

"She's bird-watching *again*!" Stephanie muttered. "I know Patti's interested in nature, but this is getting to be too much! Look at her."

But I wasn't so sure. First of all, Patti's bird book was still jammed in her pocket. And second, scrunched down behind the rock the way she was, Patti looked more like she was *hiding* than thinking about birds.

"Oh . . . h-hi, guys," Patti stammered when she saw us. She jerked the book out of her jacket pocket and started leafing through it. "I think I spotted a petrel — want to take a look?"

"No thanks," Stephanie said shortly, giving Patti a frown that meant, *What is going on?!*

But Patti only said, "How did we do in the kite contest?" as cheerfully as she could manage.

"Unfortunately, our kite got tangled up with the Tylers' — " Kate began.

" — and both kites ended up in the Atlantic," I finished for her. "And now the Tylers *really* can't stand us."

"Our kite crashed?" Patti asked.

Kate and I exchanged glances. Stephanie was still staring at Patti, who was looking very uncomfortable.

"Yeah. We lost the kite, but we did win a trophy," Kate said, holding it up so that Patti could see it.

"Neat!" Patti said. "It'll look great in the apartment, Stephanie." About the time that Stephanie's twin brother and sister were born, Stephanie's dad built this great little cottage for her in the Greens' backyard. It has pull-out couches to sleep on, a tiny refrigerator for snacks, and even a bathroom with a shower. Stephanie calls it her "apartment," and we have our sleepovers out there sometimes.

But if Patti was hoping to make Stephanie forget about her disappearing act, it didn't work.

"Where were you when we were having trouble with the kite?" Stephanie asked her sternly.

"Oh . . . uh . . . the wind had blown a lot of sand in my eyes, and I couldn't see very well," Patti fumbled, "so I . . . uh . . . ducked behind this boulder to try to get it out. . . ." She rubbed her eyes hard. "And then I spotted this petrel and . . ."

Stephanie interrupted crossly. "Let's find Nana and Dan. I'm cold, and I want to go home and sit by the fire!" Without another word, she stamped toward the cars, leaving Patti, Kate, and me to fall into line behind her.

On the way to the Kesslers', Stephanie didn't talk to Patti once. She didn't even look at her, for that matter.

When we got back to the house, Nana asked us to set the table for dinner. Kate waited until Patti was helping Nana carry some of the dishes into the dining room. Then she whispered, "Stephanie, you're giving Patti an awfully hard time. Maybe she *did* just get sand in her eyes!"

"Baloney! I think she just cares more about those dumb birds than she does about us!" Stephanie whispered back.

"And *I* think the Tyler twins make her nervous!" I said.

"They make *me* sick! But that's no excuse," Stephanie said. "She ran out on us and I just want her to be honest and tell us what's bothering her! We're supposed to tell each other everything!"

Although personally I agreed with Kate, Stephanie did have a point. Patti was acting pretty strange. After all, we're supposed to be a team, and Patti *had* left the kite contest just when we needed her most.

I hoped Mindy Sue was having more fun sleeping over at Jane Pinter's house that night than the four of us were having at the Kesslers'. Dinner was glum. Nobody really talked except Dan and Nana, and I could tell they were wondering what was wrong with us. At least the food was good — Nana had made chicken and dumplings and apple pandowdy, but even *my* appetite just wasn't its usual self.

When dinner was over, nobody wanted to hang around the big warm woodstove in the living room and talk, either. Instead, Kate, Stephanie, Patti, and I said good-night to the Kesslers and silently climbed the stairs.

"I'm beat," Stephanie announced once we'd made it to the attic room. "Who wants the bed and who wants the pull-out couch?"

"Lauren and Patti had better have the bed. It's longer," Kate said. Since Patti and I are tall, we tend to hang out over the ends of short furniture.

"Fine," Stephanie said shortly, pulling out the couch. It already had sheets and blankets on it. "As soon as I brush my teeth, I'm history."

"Me, too," Kate agreed with a yawn.

And not ten minutes later, the lights were off and everybody was in bed. There were no questions, no answers, no explanations, no conversation at all. What kind of sleepover is that?!

Actually, I was pretty tired. After all, we'd gotten up at five-thirty to catch one plane and then another, then we'd driven straight to the boat races, and lost Patti, and then jumped into the kite contest, and lost Patti *and* the kite. . . . Within seconds I was fast asleep.

I don't know how long I slept. I was dreaming about the pirate ship in *The Jolly Roger*. Only this time, it was the schooner we'd seen in the village that day. And it wasn't manned by the old movie stars in ruffled shirts and twirly mustaches. This time it was manned by the Tyler twins! They were going to make us all walk the plank. Kate first, then Stephanie, and then me. I had just been led to the edge of a board that poked out over the ocean. Fred was about to shove me into shark-infested waters and I was trembling. "No!" I shouted. "No!"

. . . And I woke up! I *was* trembling! And why not? The window closest to my head was open, and that cold Maine wind was blowing right on me, practically lifting the blankets off the bed. I looked around. Stephanie and Kate were both fast asleep — it would take a hurricane to wake those two up! Where was Patti? When I'd dozed off, she and I had been sharing the covers, but now I was alone!

"Patti?" I called softly. I could hear the waves crashing onto the Point. And I guess that's why Patti couldn't hear *me*. She was leaning way out of the open window, into that freezing wind. And all she had on was her blue nightshirt. Wasn't she cold? I snuck a peek at her. She was staring down at the Tylers' house, and she had this weird look on her face. I guess she's really feeling rotten about the kite contest, I thought gloomily. But I didn't want to embarrass her, so I buried my head under the blankets until she climbed into bed again.

A good night's rest never hurt anybody, my grandmother always says. And everybody in the attic room did wake up in a better humor. There was actually some talk as we ate breakfast — scrambled eggs and fresh cinnamon rolls that Nana had baked.

"I've watched a few sand castle experts in my time," Dan said, pouring himself a cup of coffee. "The first thing you do is dig up a lot of wet sand with big shovels. Then you have to move it higher up on the beach, past the tide line."

"Or the high tide will wash it all away, right?" Kate asked.

Dan nodded. "The tide comes in, your castle goes out," he said. "Okay — then, you pile the wet sand into a large mound. That's what you'll carve your sand castle from."

All four of us nodded. Patti was paying as close attention as Kate, Stephanie, and I.

"Then it's time to make the most important decision: Do you want to start at the top of the mound and work down, or at the bottom and work up?" said Dan.

"Which is better?" Patti asked.

"If you're building a giant castle, it's best to start at the top, because you'll probably have to step on the bottom parts to reach it," Dan told us. "You can fix any holes or dents you might have made in the sides and bottom as you work your way down. With a smaller castle, either end is fine."

"The bigger, the better," I said, determined to win round two of our feud with the terrible Tyler twins.

"Absolutely. After all, there are *four* of us," Stephanie said, with a pointed glance at Patti.

"We're a team!" said Kate.

And we were a team, for a while, anyway. We dug around in Nana's kitchen cabinets and closets, and came up with all sorts of good things for shaping the sand: two rubber buckets, an ice-cream scoop, spoons in different sizes, a couple of spatulas, a plastic knife, and a few forks. Dan brought up three big shovels from the basement for us, and dragged a small wheelbarrow out of the garage. We loaded all of our equipment into the back of the Jeep station wagon. Then Nana and Dan and the four of us headed for the beach again.

"Uh-oh — early birds," Stephanie murmured as we rolled up to the edge of the sand.

The Tyler twins had beaten us to it! They were way down the beach, already hard at work on a big mound of sand almost as tall as they were. I glanced at Patti, but she didn't show any signs of disappearing.

"Our castle will be twice as big and twice as

good as theirs," Kate said firmly. "Come on, team, let's get moving!"

Wet sand is *seriously* heavy. But Dan did a lot of the work, including most of the shoveling. He also rolled the sand-filled wheelbarrow up to the spot we'd chosen, which was right next to a twisted piece of silvery driftwood, eight or nine times, at least. When he'd moved enough sand, he went back to the Jeep to drink some of the hot chocolate Nana had brought with her, and left us to ourselves.

We sank down on our knees and started shaping the huge pile of wet sand into a giant cone.

"This is perfect, don't you think?" Kate said, smoothing out the sand in front of her. "This driftwood will look like the trunk of an ancient tree that's toppled over beside the castle. Remember that castle in *The Barbarians*?" That's another old movie we've all seen a dozen times.

"Sure, the one with lots of neat-looking towers and turrets and walls. Hey — we could even have a drawbridge!" Stephanie said. "I think there are some pieces of wood lying around Dan's garage. One of them's bound to be the right size."

"We could make it a castle on its own little island!" Patti suggested excitedly. "We could scoop out a small lake around it, and fill it with water from the ocean. . . ."

"That's a great idea!" Stephanie said, beaming at Patti approvingly. She gave the mound of sand a final pat. "Now that we've taken care of the basic shape, how do we want to handle the top? A bunch of smaller towers? Or should we go for a single *humongous* one? We could use one of these buckets to mold it. . . ."

"Hi-i-yee!" A voice floated toward us on the wind.

"Hi!" Stephanie yelled back. "It's Mindy Sue and Jane!" she said to us — she was the only one facing in their direction.

Kate and I swiveled around to wave to them, too. When we turned back to the mound, Patti was gone! *Again!*

But not completely, this time. "There she is!" said Kate. "She's headed down the beach *toward* those horrible Tyler twins!"

If she wasn't hiding from the twins, what *was* she doing? Chasing a bird? The back of Patti's plaid jacket bobbed up and down as she sprinted away from us without so much as a backward glance!

"Patti!" Stephanie bellowed. "You come back here!"

Patti didn't even slow down.

"This is ridiculous!" Stephanie fumed. "She probably just spotted some dumb old petals that she wanted to check out up close!"

"Petrels. . . ," Kate said absently.

"Petals, petrels," Stephanie said. "Whatever they're called, those birds are obviously a lot more important to Patti Jenkins right now than the Sleep-over Friends are!"

I still couldn't believe Patti was acting this way, but who could argue with the facts? Patti veered away from the twins, toward a gray-and-white rock.

"See?" Stephanie said. "That's probably where their nest is. . . ."

Then Mindy Sue and Jane walked up to us from the opposite direction.

"Didn't I see somebody tear away from here?" Mindy Sue asked, after she and Jane had checked out our castle-to-be.

"Patti," Kate replied gloomily.

"I *still* haven't even met her," Mindy Sue pointed out.

"No, and you probably won't!" Stephanie said bitterly. "She's too busy chasing after birds!"

"Birds?" Mindy Sue said.

"Like right now," Stephanie said. "She's behind

53

that rock, making the acquaintance of some petrels!"

"Uh-uh." Jane Pinter shook her head.

"Uh-uh?" I said.

"No way," Jane said firmly. "My mom's crazy about birds, and I've picked up a little bit about them from her. This is definitely the wrong time of year for petrels and most of the other shore birds. They're all out at sea."

Jane sounded like she knew what she was talking about. But if Patti wasn't chasing birds, what *was* she doing?

Chapter 6

Stephanie was wondering the same thing. "Why would Patti make up the stuff about petrels?" she burst out once Mindy Sue and Jane had left us to pick out the site for their sand castle. "Why is she acting so *weird*?"

"Maybe Patti's bored hanging around with us, so she cuts out every time she gets a chance?" I suggested.

"Lau-ren, that doesn't make any sense. She'd do it all the time then," Kate said sensibly. "Why only in Maine?"

"Maybe she really wants to see a petrel or a shearwater or something and she wants to be on the spot in case one lands," said Stephanie.

"Maybe . . ." Kate said doubtfully.

But we soon found out *that* wasn't it, either. We were just sitting there, on the beach, staring blankly at the big pile of wet sand that was supposed to be a castle, and trying to figure out what was really going on with Patti, when Dan walked up.

"Your grandmother's driving Patti home in the Jeep," Dan said to Stephanie. "Patti's not feeling well. So I thought I'd come down here and give out free castle advice — and hot chocolate — until she gets back."

But Patti didn't come back. And when Nana took us home for lunch, we found her lying in the spare bedroom on the second floor, with the curtains drawn.

"Sssh! Don't bother her," Nana told us. "She has a terrible headache."

Patti didn't even come down to eat with us. Instead, Nana took a bowl of soup up to her room. And when we went back to our sand castle that afternoon, Patti stayed in bed.

Still, even though there were only three of us on the job, we got a lot done. Our castle really started to take shape. It had a huge tower at the top, and then lots of walls and smaller towers as we moved down the sides.

The Tyler twins were back at work, too. They were too far away for us to see what their castle looked like, but we could tell it was *big*. And by the time their dad came to get them, they'd carved the whole top half of it.

Other groups were scattered here and there across the beach, but Mindy Sue and Jane were closest to us. Their castle was smaller, and they'd almost finished it when Nana arrived.

"I told your mother I'd be glad to give you and Jane a ride to your house," Nana said to Mindy Sue. "She's still busy setting up for the dance this evening."

"What are you guys going to wear tonight?" Stephanie eagerly asked the two of them as we all squeezed into the Jeep.

"Sweaters and jeans," Mindy Sue replied.

Stephanie looked a little disappointed.

"I'm afraid it's strictly informal," Nana said with a laugh. She turned the car around and headed up the gravel road.

"I think I'll wear my denim skirt and purple tights," Kate said.

"I brought my new turquoise sweatshirt with the pink and yellow splotches on it," I said.

"And I've got my red-and-black striped wool pants," said Stephanie.

"Isn't Patti coming?" Mindy Sue asked. "I'm beginning to think she's a real mystery woman!''

We're beginning to think so, too! I thought to myself.

"Do you think Patti *will* come, Nana?" Stephanie asked her grandmother.

"We'll have to see how she feels," Nana replied, turning the Jeep off the gravel road and bumping toward the tip of the Point. "If Patti still isn't feeling well, she and I will stay home, and Dan will drive the rest of you girls to the dance."

And *I* believe that's the only reason Patti decided she'd go — she didn't want to ruin a good time for Nana and Dan. She sure wasn't happy about it, though. When we got to the Island Community Center — a large, plain, one-story building behind the post office — Patti sort of hung back at the door. Kate finally had to grab the sleeve of her jacket and drag her inside with the rest of us.

Patti must have felt a little better once she got inside, though. There was so much going on that it was easy to get lost in the crowd if you wanted to. Folding chairs lined the walls, some empty, some taken by people talking and laughing. There was a long refreshment table in one corner of the room, with two kinds of punch, and all kinds of cakes, cookies, and other snacks. A funny three-piece band with a fiddle, an accordian, and a bass, was playing, and most of Crab Island was whirling around the floor to a polka. Grown-ups were dancing with grown-ups, kids with kids, kids with grown-ups, *little* kids with grown-ups — even the Tyler twins were getting down on the sidelines.

"There's Mindy Sue!" Stephanie exclaimed. Mindy Sue was wheeling around with a thin blond boy with a nice smile. And we'd barely taken ten steps into the room ourselves when Dan whirled Nana away to the music. Then an old guy with a beard — he turned out to be Miss Bessie's husband — asked Kate to dance. A seventh-grader, one of the Washburn boys — the ones who'd won the "Most Unusual" kite prize — asked Stephanie to dance. And I ended up with a very short fifth-grader named Josh Levy.

Josh Levy . . . the name sounded familiar. "Didn't you win thirty points in the kite contest?" I asked the top of his dark brown head, which was about all I could see as we reeled around to the polka.

"Yeah, my sister Becky and I won first," Josh replied, looking up at me just long enough to step on my toes. "Sorry," he said when I yelped. "She's over there, dancing with Rob Tyler.''

"Robert Tyler?" I said as Josh stepped down *hard* on most of my foot. "Ouch!"

"Wow! Sorry!" he said. "I'm not usually so — ''

"Don't worry about it," I said. "It's not your fault. Where is your sister Becky?"

Josh pointed and there she was all right, twirling around and around the floor with Robert Tyler. Robert was wearing a green-and-black plaid shirt, faded jeans, and loafers, and he looked totally fabulous. Somehow I couldn't believe the twins would *ever* look that good!

Becky Levy was a small, dainty girl, with pink cheeks and curly dark hair. She had on a hot pink blazer, black jeans, and black sneakers with lime-green laces. Very hot. And she and Robert were smiling at each other like they were the only people in the world. The cutest guy on the island was clearly taken.

"They seem to like each other," I said.

"Yeah." Josh lowered his voice. "It's sort of a secret . . . but they're kind of going steady."

"Wow!" I said. What great island gossip!

Josh made a motion across his mouth that meant

"zip your lips." When I nodded, he added in a murmur, "Our parents think Becky's too young to focus on one guy, so she and Rob have to be cool about it."

As far as I was concerned, their smiles were announcing it to all of Crab Island. I couldn't wait to tell Stephanie, Patti, and Kate the news. But where were they? At last, I spotted the back of Kate's blonde head across the dance floor. Then I saw Stephanie twirling past Josh and me with the Washburn boy. But what about Patti? Was she gone again? This disappearing business was getting to be a *very* tiresome habit!

"Excuse me. I just remembered something I have to ask Stephanie," I said to Josh. I reached out and caught the back of Stephanie's black sweater just before she reeled out of range.

"Lau-ren!" she said crossly, lurching to a halt.

"We have to talk," I said so seriously that Stephanie didn't make me explain myself, for once.

"Okay," she agreed. She turned to the tall seventh-grader she'd been dancing with. "Thanks for the dance, Andrew."

"Don't you think he's cute? *I* do!" she whispered to me as she followed me off the dance floor. "Did you have to cut in? I was having fun!"

"Sorry," I said, pushing her onto a folding chair and flopping down next to her. "But it's important. Have you seen Patti?"

But Stephanie didn't hear me because she was busy asking, "Who's the girl that Robert Tyler is being so cozy with?"

"Becky Levy. She won the kite contest, remember? And her little brother just told me that she and Robert are practically going steady!" I said.

"Really? He's *so* good-looking," Stephanie said, staring at them. "Where is Patti?" she asked suddenly.

"That's what I wanted to talk to you about!" I replied. "I think she dropped off the face of the earth right after we saw the Tyler twins!"

Stephanie nodded knowingly. "I think I'm beginning to get it," she said.

"You are?" I asked, because I still wasn't sure I did.

"What's going on?" Kate dropped onto the chair on the other side of Stephanie. "Whew!" She fanned her face with her hands. " 'Mr. Bessie' " is quite a dancer!"

"This is serious, Kate!" Stephanie said. "Patti's missing again."

"Oh, no!" Kate peered quickly around the room.

"We've already looked," I told her.

"She's in the car," Kate guessed. "And we're cornering her, right now!"

The three of us rushed outside, and over to Main Street. The Kesslers' Jeep was parked under the street lamp in front of the General Store. And sure enough, Patti was huddled in the back seat.

Kate and I slid in beside her. Stephanie climbed into the front. Then she leaned over the seat to say, "Patti, we know what's been bothering you."

"You do?!" Patti sounded totally shocked.

"Sure. It's the Tyler twins," Stephanie said. "They make you remember all the bad stuff that happened when you were a new kid, right?"

"The Tyler twins?" Patti groaned and shook her head.

"It's not them?!" I said. "Then what *is* the matter, Patti?"

"Come on!" said Kate. "It's all for one and one for all, isn't it?" That's a motto we borrowed from *The Three Musketeers* for the Sleepover Friends.

"Ye-es," Patti said slowly.

"So what are you upset about? Or who?" Kate asked.

"Patti . . ." Stephanie prodded.

Patti took a deep breath. "Mindy Sue Watson," she mumbled at last.

"Mindy Sue Watson?!" Kate, Stephanie, and I sqawked at the same time.

On the one hand, it didn't make any sense at all. On the other hand, I realized slowly, it *did* fit. The first time Patti disappeared was when Mindy Sue showed up at the pier in the village with her mom. The second time was at the kite contest, when Mindy Sue and Jane dashed past us with their kite. The third time was this morning at the beach, when Mindy Sue and Jane hurried toward us from their car. And tonight Patti had vanished as soon as we stepped through the door at the Community Center, and Stephanie said, "There's Mindy Sue!"

"But why?" Kate said to Patti. "She seems like a really nice person."

"Besides, even if she weren't, she hasn't had a chance to do anything mean," Stephanie said.

"We never even met her until yesterday," I pointed out.

"But *I* have," Patti said quietly.

Chapter
7

"You know Mindy Sue Watson?!" Stephanie said. "How?"

"We were in third grade together at The Day School," Patti answered. "And it was the worst year of my life."

"Because of Mindy Sue?" I asked.

Patti nodded. "She made fun of me every chance she got."

"Saying what?" Kate asked.

Patti sighed. "She said that I was too tall, I was too skinny, I was a bookworm, I was a baby, that nobody would ever like me because I was such a geek." Patti shrugged helplessly. "I was afraid to tell you guys because I thought you might think it over and agree with her," she added in a small voice.

"Patti! Give us some credit as friends, okay?!" Stephanie said. "Besides, it sounds to me as if Mindy Sue was just jealous of you."

"Jealous of me? Why should she have been?" Patti asked.

"Plenty of reasons. Because you were smart," Kate began, "and maybe you were taller than she was. Was she short in third grade?"

Patti nodded.

"Maybe she was a little chubby, too," I said.

"Kind of," Patti said, and grinned for the first time in ages. "And not very good at games."

"Jealousy," Stephanie said. "Pure and simple."

"It still hurt," Patti murmured.

"But people can change," I told Patti, remembering what Mindy Sue herself had said about the Tyler twins. Borrowing it, I added, "I think Mindy Sue *has* improved with age, Patti."

Stephanie nodded in agreement. "Yeah, Patti, third grade was a long time ago. You shouldn't still be upset about that stuff. Why don't you come back to the dance with us? We'll re-introduce the two of you, and you'll see that she's really okay now."

"Or I'll jump on her case!" Kate growled fiercely as a joke.

Stephanie and I giggled, but Patti shook her

66

head. "Uh-uh. You guys go back. I'll stay here until you're ready to go home. I brought along my bird book" — she pulled it out of her jacket pocket and held it up to the light from the street lamp — "I'll be fine."

And there was no budging her. She even made us promise not to tell Nana and Dan.

So Kate, Stephanie, and I did go back to the Community Center, and we did have fun. Stephanie got to dance with Andrew Washburn again, and she told me she thought he was almost as cute as Robert Tyler! "I know he's nothing like Tommy Hepp," she sighed, "but don't you think he looks kind of like . . . Kevin DeSpain?" I danced a couple of careful polkas with Josh Levy, who I decided wasn't bad — for a short guy. And Kate danced with everybody — Dan, "Mr. Bessie," even a quick round with Robert Tyler! But even with all the excitement, the idea of Patti sitting all by herself in the cold car was always lurking in a corner of our minds.

After a while, Nana noticed that Patti was missing again. She made up her mind we'd all better go home. We found our coats and headed for the door. But Mindy Sue caught up with us. "Would you like to come to my house for breakfast tomorrow?" she asked.

Stephanie, Kate, and I looked at each other. I mean, no matter how hard we'd tried to convince Patti otherwise, we were definitely feeling a little funny about Mindy Sue ourselves at this point. All for one, and one for all?

"Uh . . . we have to . . . uh —" Stephanie began.

Mindy Sue cut in with, "Why don't you call me when you wake up in the morning? You can decide then."

As we trudged back to the Jeep behind Nana and Dan, Kate murmured, "Now what?"

"We can't go without Patti," Stephanie said. "We'll just have to think of some excuse for Mindy Sue, like you sprained your ankle on the stairs, Kate. Or Lauren's coming down with the flu."

"And then we show up at the beach to finish our sand castle, feeling fine?" Kate snorted.

"Hmmm. That *is* a problem," Stephanie admitted. "So what *do* we do?"

When we got home, we talked a little more to Patti about it. But she stood firm. She was not going to let Mindy Sue have the opportunity for a face-to-face meeting, even though we tried to tell her there was no way Mindy Sue would give her a hard time. "That third-grade stuff is history!" Stephanie told her.

But Patti just shook her head. She would get through the next day somehow. And Monday we were flying back to Riverhurst.

"I don't want to wreck Nana's fun tomorrow," Patti said. "So I plan to do lots of bird-watching from behind large rocks." And that was that!

At least, that would have been that, if Mother Nature hadn't stepped in.

In the middle of the night, when all four of us were sound asleep in our room in the attic, there was suddenly an incredible *CRASH* outside the house! It was so loud that Patti and I both shot out of bed. Even Kate and Stephanie woke up!

"Wh-what's *that?*" Stephanie mumbled.

In the next second we knew. There was a brilliant flash of lightning, followed by a deafening crash of thunder.

"Wow!" said Stephanie, wide awake now. "That was awfully close!"

"Listen to the wind!" I said. It was absolutely howling around the attic room, making all the windows rattle and shake. Then the rain began, great sheets of it, pounding against the roof.

"Weather!" Kate groaned sleepily, burrowing under the covers again.

"Mmm," said Stephanie. She yawned loudly. " 'Night." And she plumped the pillow over her head to block out the noise.

Patti and I shrugged at each other and got back into bed, too. I fell asleep to the gurgle of rain running down the window next to our bed.

When we got up the next morning, though, the sun was shining brightly. The wind had died altogether and the ocean was sparkling and calm.

"What a beautiful day!" Stephanie exclaimed as we trotted downstairs to breakfast. "Hi, Nana, Dan. Isn't it gorgeous out?" she added as we walked into the kitchen.

"I'm afraid Dan has some bad news for you girls," Nana said.

"What kind of bad news?" Stephanie asked, her smile fading.

"Mike Watson and I drove over to the beach very early this morning to see if the sand castles survived the storm," Dan said, shaking his head. "I'm afraid that during the storm last night, the tide was really high, and a good many of the castles were washed away."

"Everyone's?" Kate asked.

"Well, yours, and Mindy Sue's, and the Tyler

twins', too. The poor little fellows were practically in tears. They needed lots of points for their castle to help them win that Sunfish," Dan said.

"You see, the Tyler boys are crazy about sailing," Nana explained quietly. "I think they were really counting on getting that Sunfish somehow, and now . . ."

"When is the judging?" I asked.

"One-thirty," Dan said.

"We definitely don't have time to start from scratch," Stephanie said. "It's almost nine already."

"Could we at least go to the beach?" Kate asked.

"I'll take you right now, if you'd like," Dan said.

We grabbed some of Nana's fresh-out-of-the-oven cranberry muffins off a platter on the counter, rushed out to the garage, and jumped into the Jeep — even Patti!

"Who put the tools in here?" Kate asked, because the back of the station wagon was crammed with shovels, rakes, the little wheelbarrow, and all our other stuff.

"Oh, I did," Dan said apologetically. "I thought you just might want to make another castle."

Stephanie shook her head. "Uh-uh," she said glumly. "It's too late for the three of us to build anything. . . ."

71

"I'll help," Patti piped up from the second seat.

Stephanie whirled around to stare at her. "You will? But Mindy Sue might be there."

"I don't care," said Patti. "We're a team, aren't we?"

Sleepover Friends forever! "Way to go!" I murmured.

"We can do it!" said Kate. "Watch out, world! Here come the future sand-castle champions of Crab Island!"

When we got to the beach, though, we changed our minds pretty quickly.

"There's absolutely nothing left!" Stephanie wailed. "I thought at least *part* of our mound would still be here. But even the driftwood's gone!"

"Washed out to sea," Dan said.

The beach had been scoured by the storm. A couple of sand castles, the ones that had been built on the far edge of the beach, had made it through the night — but they were in pretty bad shape. The rain had kind of melted them down, until they looked more like ancient ruins or piles of rubble than medieval castles.

"Isn't this the *worst*?!" someone called out from behind us.

"Patti, it's Mindy Sue," Kate warned. Mindy Sue

and Jane Pinter had just climbed out of Mr. Watson's car, and were hurrying toward us.

"If you want to split, go ahead," Stephanie said to Patti in a low voice. "We'll understand."

But Patti shook her head, and stood her ground.

"I'm so upset!" Mindy Sue exclaimed when she got to us. "Isn't this awful? Not one ounce of sand to show for all that hard work!" Then she noticed that there were four of us. "You must be . . ."

"This is Patti Jenkins," Stephanie said.

"Hi, Patti, I've been dying to meet you. I'm Mindy Sue Watson." Clearly, Mindy Sue didn't remember Patti at all!

Patti could have let it slide. But instead, she said bravely, "Yes, I know. We were both in Mrs. Quinn's class at The Day School."

"Patti Jenkins?!" Mindy Sue shrieked. "Patti!" She gave a very startled Patti a big hug. Then she turned to Stephanie, Kate, and me and said, "You know I was so *jealous* of this girl! She was the smartest kid in the whole school, she was tall — I was a total shrimp — our teacher loved her. She had everything! I can't believe I didn't recognize you, Patti! It's so great to see you again!" And she obviously meant it!

"It's good to see you, too, Mindy Sue," Patti said, looking pleased and surprised because *she*

73

meant it, too. I think she realized that maybe she had kind of overreacted. Mindy Sue really was different, and all that old third-grade stuff didn't matter anymore. Kate, Stephanie, and I looked at each other and smiled. People *can* change!

"So what are we going to do about the contest?" Kate asked, to bring us back to the present.

"I have an idea," said Patti. "What if all of us join forces —"

"Great!" said Stephanie. "Twelve hands have got to be better than eight."

But Patti wasn't finished yet. "— with them," she went on, pointing farther down the beach. Two small figures were standing close together, shoulders slumped, heads down.

"Join forces with the terrible Tyler twins?!" I yelped. But they *did* look sort of pathetic.

"We don't really care if we win this contest or not," Patti said. "But they *do*. Dan and Nana told us how much that Sunfish means to them."

Kate, Stephanie, and I slowly nodded.

"Patti's right," Mindy Sue said after a pause. "Look at those poor things."

Fred had draped his arm around John's shoulder, as if he was trying to cheer him up.

"Let's go talk to them," Stephanie said. So the six of us headed down the beach.

The Tyler twins weren't exactly thrilled to see us at first. "What do *you* want?" Fred asked rudely.

"Come to laugh at us?" John asked suspiciously.

And when we told them about Patti's idea, their immediate reaction was, *"No way!"*

"What if by some weird coincidence the castle won?" John said. "We'd have to share our boat with six girls!"

"Four of us will hardly ever be here," Patti pointed out.

"And I'm only on the islands on weekends, mostly," Mindy Sue said. "Anyway, my family already has a boat."

Fred turned to his brother. "Come on," he said, "they're right. I mean, Jane lives here, but we're used to her." They're all in the same class at Crab Island Elementary.

And that's how the eight of us ended up making possibly the most special sand castle of all time. Eight people have eight different approaches, and eight times as many terrific ideas. Like Fred's.

"Why don't we make it a castle on a planet in outer space?" he suggested, once we'd pushed twelve wheelbarrow loads of wet sand into a gigantic pile. "Like the castle in that movie, *The Black Knights of Altair Three?*"

"Fantastic!" said Patti, who loves science fiction herself. "We'll have towers and turrets and walls, like in a regular castle, but we'll make them sort of streamlined and super modern."

"Right!" said John. "Maybe this won't be so bad, after all," he admitted. "Hand me that big spoon, Mindy Sue, please. Patti and I are gonna start at the top!"

Chapter
8

We finished our space castle with twenty minutes to spare, and it was wonderful-looking! It was my height, and twice as long as it was tall. Ramps crisscrossed the castle from one arched doorway to another. It had fifteen towers of all sizes, and lots of round windows. It even had a flat launching pad for spaceships, like the one in *Altair Three*. Fred and Patti made a flying saucer from the big pottery plate on which Nana had brought us our lunch of ham sandwiches.

"It's perfect!" Stephanie exclaimed, once we'd put down our tools and had time to back away and really look at our work. "Totally optimo!"

"Dyno-mite!" John agreed.

"But check out our competition!" Fred said nervously. "The Ellisons' castle is as big as ours, with a lot more stuff on it." He pointed at one of the castles that had made it through the storm. The two Ellison boys — one's in sixth grade, the other's in eighth grade — were still carving designs on it with plastic knives, and it was absolutely covered with turrets and towers.

"They've already got thirty points for their boat race," Fred added gloomily.

"It looks like a pincushion," Kate said critically about the Ellisons' castle.

"And the Levys'," said John. The Levys were about twenty yards down the beach, putting the finishing touches on what looked like a monster mansion. And who was helping them? Robert Tyler!

"That fink!" Fred muttered.

"No contest," Mindy Sue said firmly. "There's nothing *different* about their castles."

I guess that's what the judge thought, too. He was a real architect, from Boston. And he seemed to take forever studying each of the sand castles on the beach — there were sixteen of them altogether. Still, ours was the only one he looked at twice. Finally, he walked over to Mr. Fenton, who turned out to be in charge of the castle contest, too.

"I think he's made up his mind," Patti whispered excitedly.

"We want that boat, we want that boat. . . ." Fred and John Tyler began chanting in a low voice.

"I have the results of the sand-castle competition for you!" Mr. Fenton boomed so suddenly that Mindy Sue and I jumped. He clambered up on a big gray rock and continued. "Without further ado, third prize in the sand-castle contest goes to Mary Rose Raynor and Carolyn Gray!" They were little kids, around eight years old, and their parents went wild with applause. "They'll win ten points toward the Sunfish, and a very pretty trophy that is now on display at the Community Center!"

Mr. Fenton cleared his throat and began again. "Second prize . . ." We all held our breath, because if we won second, and the Ellisons or the Levys won first, the Sunfish would be theirs. Both groups already had thirty points, like the Tyler twins. Everything was riding on who won best sand castle!

"Second prize . . ."

"He is so slow!" Patti murmured anxiously.

". . . goes to the Ellisons! Jerry and Nathan. Twenty points and a trophy. Congratulations, boys!"

The Ellisons said "thank you" politely enough,

but they frowned in our direction. The Sunfish could still be theirs, if we — or the Levys — didn't win first place.

"Cross your fingers," said Kate.

"The first prize, for thirty points and-a-beautiful-trophy-that-you-can-pick-up-at-the-Community Center —" Mr. Fenton ran his words together in a hurry, and then paused again. He beamed at the crowd on the beach. All eight of us crossed our fingers. "First prize goes to *the Tyler twins and their group!*"

We yelled so long and so loud that I thought I'd lose my voice!

But Mr. Fenton was holding his hands for silence. "Mr. DePalma, an architect as well as our judge, wants me to commend you on your imagination and your originality!"

"YO! Way to go!" Fred and John gave each other a high-five, and then gave one to each of us girls.

"That does it, folks!" said Mr. Fenton. "See you at the clambake!"

Mmmmmmmmmm-mm, the clambake! That was definitely a high spot of *my* first visit to Maine. As soon as Mr. Fenton stepped down from his perch on the rock, Dan and Mr. Watson and a bunch of the grown-ups dug a big pit in the sand not far from our castle. All us kids helped them line the pit with rocks. Then we collected driftwood for the fire they'd be building at the bottom of the pit.

To have a real Maine clambake, you let the fire blaze for a while, until it burns down to white-hot coals. Then you pile in the food. Clams, of course, potatoes, apples, chickens, hamburgers, mussels, crabs, lobsters, hot dogs, sausages . . . I could go on and on!

Once we'd put all the food on the fire, we gathered as much seaweed as we could find. We packed the seaweed over and around the food in the pit to steam it. Then we settled down and waited for everything to cook. We sang songs and told ghost stories. And when they finally pulled off the seaweed, that food smelled better than practically anything I've ever smelled in my life! And tasted better, too. Or, as Patti put it, "It's a feast fit for a king! Which is only right with all these castles around!"

Mindy Sue and Jane sat with us at the clambake, of course. And so did the Tyler twins. I wasn't sure if it was because they really wanted to, or because they thought they owed us one.

But then the boys showed up early the next morning, along with Mindy Sue, to see us off. Nana

and Dan had decided they'd drive us to Portland —
that way, I'd only have to worry about *one* plane
ride — so we had to catch the car ferry.

We said our good-byes, traded addresses, then
stuffed our luggage into the back of the Jeep, and
climbed in ourselves.

"We're going to mail you the castle trophy,"
Fred said through the open car window.

"Why us?" Stephanie asked.

"It was you guys who came up with the idea to
build a sand castle together," John said gruffly. "We
wouldn't have won the Sunfish without you."

"It was really Patti's idea," Kate said, to set the
record straight.

"Patti's always had great ideas!" Mindy Sue
said, reaching through the window to give Patti a
hug. "Let's not lose touch again, okay? I'll write you
soon."

"Good-bye! 'Bye!" we called out the window as
we rolled away from the Kesslers' house.

"We'll teach you to sail the next time you
come!" Fred yelled.

"Yeah! Remember, it's your boat, too!" John
shouted.

"So you see, Patti," Stephanie said as we all

squeezed together in the second seat, "new kids aren't always so awful."

"Or old kids, either," said Patti with a smile. She was looking down at the piece of paper Mindy Sue had handed her, with her address on it.

"On the other hand," I said, settling back, "nothing's quite as good as the Sleepover Friends!"

#28 Lauren's New Address

Dad kept driving until he reached Brio Drive.

Brio Drive is a long, winding road that ends practically in farm country. And that's where he finally stopped, almost at the end of the road, in front of a big, gloomy old house. It looked a lot like "Nightmare Mansion," which they always show at the beginning of "Friday Night Chillers" on Channel 21.

Dad unbuckled his seat belt and climbed out of the car. Mom was right behind him.

Roger and the four of us just sat where we were. Then Dad said, "Well, jump out! This is it!"

"This is *what*, Dad?" Roger said grouchily.

"Our new house!" Dad replied, looking pleased as punch.

WIN A 10-SPEED BIKE!

Enter the

SLEEPOVER FRIENDS™
Ultimate Sleepover Giveaway!

Can you describe the ULTIMATE sleepover? Fill in the coupon below with your
answers and you can win the ULTIMATE
prize—a 10-Speed bike! Return by
November 30, 1990.

25 Second Prize Winners get sleeping bags!

Rules: Entries must be postmarked by November 30, 1990. Winners will be picked at random and notified by mail. No purchase necessary. Void where prohibited. Taxes on prizes are the responsibility of the winners and their immediate families. Employees of Scholastic Inc.; its agencies, affiliates, subsidiaries; and their immediate families not eligible. For a complete list of winners, send a self-addressed stamped envelope to Sleepover Friends Ultimate Sleepover Giveaway, Giveaway Winners List, at the address provided below.

Fill in the coupon below or write the information on a 3" x 5" piece of paper and mail to: SLEEPOVER FRIENDS ULTIMATE SLEEPOVER GIVEAWAY, Scholastic Inc., P.O. Box 754, 730 Broadway, New York, NY 10003. Canadian residents send entries to: Iris Ferguson, Scholastic Inc., 123 Newkirk Road, Richmond Hill, Ontario, Canada L4C365.

- -

Sleepover Friends Ultimate Sleepover Giveaway
Just fill in the blanks!

The ULTIMATE SLEEPOVER would be on a _____ night.
(pick a day)

We'd eat _____ , listen to _____ ,
(food)   *(favorite music)*

talk all night about _____ , watch
(fun topic)

_____ , and play _____ .
(movie/TV show)   *(name of game)*

Name _____ Age _____

Street _____

City _____ State _____ Zip _____

SLE290

Pack your bags for fun and adventure with

SLEEPOVER FRIENDS™

by Susan Saunders

America's Favorite Series

THE BABY-SITTERS CLUB

by Ann M. Martin

Collect Them All!

The seven girls at Stoneybrook Middle School get into all kinds of adventures...with school, boys, and, of course, baby-sitting!

For a complete listing of all the Baby-sitter Club titles write to :
Customer Service at the address below.

Available wherever you buy books...or use the coupon below.